Simon James is an award-winning author and illustrator of books for children and is a regular speaker in schools and at festivals across the UK and the US. His books include *Frog and Beaver*, *Rex*, *Nurse Clementine*, *George Flies South*, *Dear Greenpeace*, *Leon and Bob*, *Sally and the Limpet* and the bestselling Baby Brains series. Simon likes to draw with a dip pen and uses watercolour paints for his illustrations. To find out more about Simon James and his books, visit **www.simonjamesbooks.com**

For Laura and for Emily – with gratitude

First published 2017 by Walker Books Ltd, 87 Vauxhall Walk, London SE11 5HJ

2 4 6 8 10 9 7 5 3 1

© 2017 Simon James

The right of Simon James to be identified as author/illustrator of this work has been asserted by him in accordance with the Copyright, Designs and Patents Act 1988

This book has been typeset in Goudy

Printed in China

British Library Cataloguing in Publication Data:
a catalogue record for this book is available from the British Library

ISBN 978-1-4063-7410-0

www.walker.co.uk

WALKER BOOKS
AND SUBSIDIARIES
LONDON · BOSTON · SYDNEY · AUCKLAND

SIMON JAMES

The Boy From Mars

On the day Stanley's mum had to go away,
Stanley decided to leave Planet Earth.
"It's just for work – I'll be back tomorrow,"
said Mum. "Be good for Dad."

"Aren't you going to wave goodbye?" said Dad.
But Stanley didn't.

Stanley ran out into the garden, climbed into his
spaceship and blasted off into outer space ...

heading for Mars.

A little while later, the spaceship landed back on earth in Stanley's garden.

A small martian crawled out.

"Hello, Stanley," said Will. "Why are you wearing
that funny hat?"
"I'm not Stanley. I'm a martian," said the martian.

"Well, you look exactly like my
brother Stanley," said Will.

"Well, I'm not," insisted the martian.
"I've come to explore your sibilization.
Take me to your leader."

"Dad!" said Will. "I found a martian in the garden!"

"Hello, Martian," said Dad.
"You've arrived just in time for dinner.
Would you like to wash your hands?"

"I think you'll find martians
don't wash their hands,"
said the martian.
"Oh," said Dad.

At dinner, the martian wasn't impressed.
"Martians don't like earth food," he said.
"We don't eat rocks."
"It's not a rock," said Dad. "It's a jacket potato."

For pudding, Dad gave the
martian some ice cream.
"That's more like it,"
said the martian.

After dinner the martian helped clear the table.

"It's time for bed," said Dad. "It's school tomorrow."

"I think you'll find martians don't have bedtimes,"
said the martian.

"I think you'll find they do on earth," said Dad.

In the bathroom, Will was getting ready for bed.
"I suppose martians don't have to brush their teeth," said Will.
"That's right," said the martian. "And we don't have to
wash either."

That night, the martian slept in Stanley's bed.

Dad came upstairs to tuck him in.

"Do martians always wear their helmets in bed?"
asked Dad.

"Always," said the martian.

"Night, night, then," sighed Dad.

The next day at school the martian
met Stanley's best friend, Josh.
"You're not a martian," said Josh.

"Yes, I am," said the martian.
"You're not," said Josh. "You're Stanley!"
"Am not!" said the martian.
"You are!" insisted Josh.

The martian was upset.
He pushed Josh away!

Josh burst into tears and
ran off to tell the teacher.

After saying sorry to Josh, the martian spent the rest
of the morning sitting outside the headteacher's office,
thinking about his behaviour.

"Miss Cosmos told me what happened today,"
said Dad on the way home from school.
The martian was silent.
"I wonder what Mum will think when she gets
home tonight," said Dad.

That evening, Will and the
martian heard the front door
open and raced downstairs.

"Mum!" said Will. "We missed you!"

"I missed you too," said Mum. "What have you been up to?"

"Well, we've had a martian living with us," said Will.
"Look, here he is!"

"Hello there," said Mum. "Have you
been a good little martian?"

The little martian froze. He didn't know what to say.
Suddenly, he turned and ran.

Out in the garden, he climbed into his spaceship
and blasted off into outer space ...

heading back to Mars.

Moments later, the spaceship landed back on earth.

Out peered
an earth boy
called Stanley.

He ran up the
steps and into
the kitchen.

"Mum, I've just got back from Mars! You wouldn't believe it," said Stanley. "They never wash, or eat their vegetables AND they're always in trouble at school!"

"Well, I'm glad you're back," said Mum. "I missed you!"
"Me too," said Stanley. "Me too."

The End